Dedicated to
Gordon MacKenzie (Uncle Gordon)
and his manuscript, Matthew's Ghost.
Thank you for inspiring us
to write our story.

www.mascotbooks.com

The Adventures of Forkman: What's That Noise?

©2021 Tiffany Caldwell & W.R. MacKenzie. All Rights Reserved. No part of this publication may be reproduced, stored in a retrieval system or transmitted in any form by any means electronic, mechanical, or photocopying, recording or otherwise without the permission of the author.

For more information, please contact:
Mascot Books
620 Herndon Parkway, Suite 320
Herndon, VA 20170
info@mascotbooks.com

Library of Congress Control Number: 2020909571

CPSIA Code: PRT0820A
ISBN-13: 978-1-64543-396-5

Printed in the United States

The Adventures of Forkman

What's That Noise?

written by

Tiffany Caldwell & W.R. MacKenzie

illustrated by Vanessa Alexandre

Chapter 3: Loading the Dishwasher

Tonight is family game night.

It is one of Kathryn and William's most favorite nights! But before they can play, there is still some work that needs to be done...

"Forkman, now that the table is cleared, what do we need to do next?" Kathryn asked.

"Well kids, it is my favorite part! It is time to load the dishwasher!" Forkman said excitedly.

"Ok!" the kids responded.

With a puzzled look on his face, William looked at Forkman and asked, "Why is loading the dishwasher your favorite part?"

With a big smile on his face, Forkman said, "I will tell you why in just a minute!"

"What do we do first, Forkman?" Kathryn asked.

"The first thing we do is rinse the plates. After they are rinsed, you place them side by side on the bottom rack of the dishwasher," explained Forkman.

DIRTY

"That seems like a great place for Pete the Plate!" William said excitedly.

"What is next?" Kathryn asked.

"Let's take any pots and pans and line them up next to Pete," Forkman said.

Kathryn and William worked together very carefully to make sure everything fit and that nothing was touching.

"What goes on the top rack of the dishwasher, Forkman?" asked William.

Forkman replied, "The top rack is used for little things, like Clara Cup and other glassware. They go along the sides. The top rack is also a great spot for any spatulas, storage containers, or small bowls."

Kathryn and William continued to work as a team to place Clara Cup and other small items on the top rack.

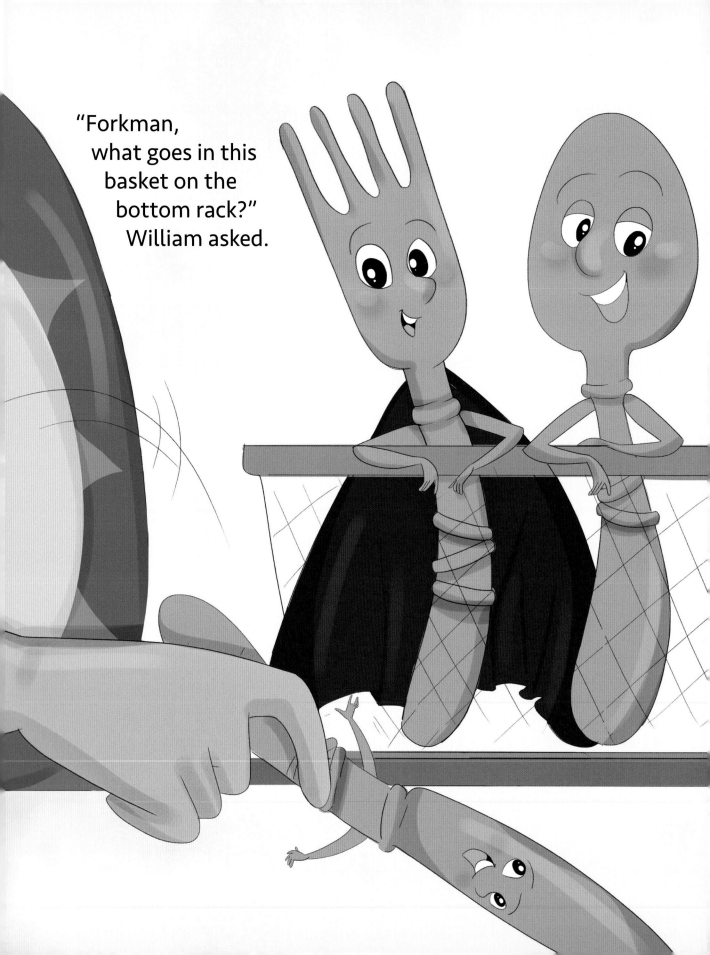

"Forkman, what goes in this basket on the bottom rack?" William asked.

Forkman looked at Kathryn and William and responded, "Remember earlier when I said loading the dishwasher was my favorite part?"

The kids looked at each other then back at Forkman and curiously said, "Yes..."

"Well kids, it is my favorite part because that is where Knifeguy, Spoondude, and I go for a bath!"

Kathryn and William started laughing as they carefully placed Forkman, Spoondude, and Knifeguy in the basket.

"Hey, William!?" Knifeguy shouted. "Can you please turn me around and put my pointy end down? I do not want anyone to get hurt by my blade!"

William followed his instructions, and the table friends were ready to go!

"Now that everything is loaded, what do we do?" Kathryn asked.

"Go ask Mom and Dad to put the detergent into the dishwasher. Those chemicals can be harmful and children should not touch them!" Forkman said.

Mom and Dad came into the kitchen and were surprised everything was done.

Kathryn and William were proud of what they had accomplished. They turned to their parents with excitement and said, "Mom! Dad! All you have to do is put in the detergent. We've done the rest!"

"Wow kids! Fabulous job! We don't know how you are learning to do all of these things, but keep up the great work!" Mom said, smiling.

"Now that the dishes are loaded, we can start our family game night! Kathryn, William, what game would you like to play?" Dad asked.

Kathryn and William looked at each other, grinning.

"Monopoly!" they said together.

Chapter 4: What's That Noise?

There are many sounds at the dinner table:
sounds of laughter, families talking, or
babies crying. While these are good sounds,
sometimes an unpleasant noise or two
slips out that should not be at the table.

Dinner was on the table and our favorite family was gathered around. William said the blessing, then they all enjoyed their meal together.

"Everything was delicious!" William said with a smile.

"Thank you, William!" Dad said.

As Mom and Dad continued to talk to Kathryn and William about their day, William let out a loud "Buuuurrppp!"

As Kathryn and William giggled, Forkman immediately stood up. Mom and Dad had shocked looks on their faces as Forkman said, "What's that noise? That sound should not be at the table!"

Buuuurrppp!

Mom and Dad asked, "Who are you?"

Kathryn said, "That is one of our table friends, Forkman!"

"Yes," said Forkman, "I have been teaching Kathryn and William the proper things to do at the table, and as silly as it may sound, burping at the table is not a proper thing to do."

"Well Forkman, it seems like you have helped the kids out before. What other noises should not be heard at the table?" Mom asked.

William answered with a giggle, "I know a sound! A toot!"

"You're right William, a toot is definitely a sound that should not be at the table," Forkman replied.

"And if you have to sneeze or blow your nose, you should always excuse yourself from the table," added Kathryn.

"You are right! And sometimes accidents happen, so if a burp or a toot accidentally slips out, the polite thing to do is to say excuse me!" Forkman said.

As the family continued to talk to Forkman, they heard a song start to play.

Kathryn, William, Mom, Forkman, and all the table friends looked at Dad and said, "What's that noise?"

Dad's face turned a little red, and Forkman hopped over to Dad and said, "One last sound we should not have at the table is a phone or any other electronic device. Put those away while we are eating. Dinner time is for the family. It is a time to talk to each other about our days or the week ahead. It is not a time to talk on the phone or play with electronics!"

Dad shut his phone off and said, "I have an idea. Let's all shut off our phones and electronics and set them in the middle of the table so no one gets the urge to look at them. That way, we can enjoy our dinner uninterrupted."

Everyone at the table promised to keep their electronics off so that they could enjoy their family dinner every night.

"Forkman, thank you for always teaching us the proper things to do!" William said.

"It's my pleasure!" Forkman replied.

"Forkman," Kathryn asked, "what are you going to teach us next?"

"Oh, you'll have to wait and see!" Forkman said with a wink.

About the Authors

W.R. MacKenzie

I retired after thirty-nine years in the bakery business. When my four children were grown, I felt it was time to share the importance of the family meal with the world. The Adventures of Forkman series teaches children how to properly conduct themselves at the table.

Our books are filled with characters all children can relate to. I believe Forkman and his pals will help children of all ages learn manners and table etiquette.

We hope you enjoy our story!

Tiffany Caldwell

I have worked with children for over fourteen years, and every year, basic manners become less evident. When I was growing up, my sisters and I took etiquette classes during the summer while we visited our grandparents. Etiquette was always a big part of our upbringing.

When we would have our family dinners, my dad, W.R. MacKenzie, would make our utensils come to life as we were eating. Forkman became a part of our dinner routine.

I am a mother of three great kids and military wife to my hero. I graduated with my bachelor's degree in 2019, and I am currently pursuing an education position in our local school district. We hope you enjoy the third and fourth chapters of The Adventures of Forkman. We are so excited to share Forkman with the world!